D1076853

R. D. BLACKMORE

Lorna Doone

Retold by John Escott

MACMILLAN READERS

BEGINNER LEVEL

Founding Editor: John Milne

The Macmillan Readers provide a choice of enjoyable reading materials for learners of English. The series is published at six levels – Starter, Beginner, Elementary, Pre-intermediate, Intermediate and Upper.

Level control

Information, structure and vocabulary are controlled to suit the students' ability at each level.

The number of words at each level:

Starter	about 300 basic words
Beginner	about 600 basic words
Elementary	about 1100 basic words
Pre-intermediate	about 1400 basic words
Intermediate	about 1600 basic words
Upper	about 2200 basic words

Vocabulary

Some difficult words and phrases in this book are important for understanding the story. Some of these words are explained in the story and some are shown in the pictures. From Pre-intermediate level upwards, words are marked with a number like this: …³. These words are explained in the Glossary at the end of the book.

Contents

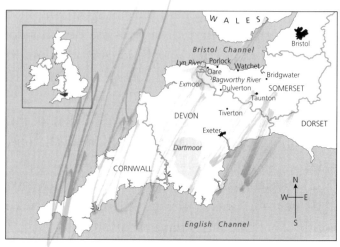

A Note About the Author

R.D. (Richard Dodderidge) **Blackmore** was born in Berkshire, England, on 7th June, 1825. His mother died a few months later.

In 1832, his father took Richard to the county of Devon, in the south-west of England. He lived there until 1843. He studied at a school in Tiverton. After that, he studied at Oxford University.

In 1852, Blackmore became a lawyer in London, and the next year he married Lucy Macguire.

Blackmore was not strong and he did not work as a lawyer for very long. He became a teacher. In 1857, Blackmore's uncle died and his money came to Richard. After that, Richard did not teach any more. He lived with his wife in a large house near London, and he wrote poems and novels. Lucy Blackmore died in 1888, and Richard died on 20th January, 1900. The Blackmores had no children.

R.D. Blackmore wrote fifteen novels. Some of these stories are: *Clara Vaughan* (1864), *Craddock Newell* (1866), *The Maid of Sker* (1872) and *Christowell* (1882). His most famous story was *Lorna Doone* (1869). It has become one of the most popular stories in English. There are many films of this story.

A Note About This Story

Time: 1673 to 1686. **Place:** Exmoor, in the south-west of England.

In the seventeenth century, most people in Britain lived in small villages. Towns and cities were small. The roads between them were bad. Journeys from the south-west of England to London were long and difficult. Travellers had to ride in coaches, or ride on horses, for several days.

There was a lot of trouble in Britain in the 1680s. Most people in the country liked King Charles II. But he died in 1685 and his brother, James, became the new king. King James II was not popular. Many powerful people in Britain wanted a different king. James Scott, Duke of Monmouth, tried to become king. His friends fought several battles with the soldiers of King James. These battles are now called the Monmouth Rebellion. The King's soldiers beat Monmouth's men. They caught the Duke of Monmouth and they killed him. The king sent a judge – George Jeffreys – to the south-west of England. Judge Jeffreys was a clever and powerful man. He killed all of Monmouth's friends.

Some of this story happens at the time of the Monmouth Rebellion. In the story, John Ridd is for King James, but John's cousin, Tom Faggus, is against the King.

Note: Bridgwater – say ˈbrɪdʒwɔːtə, Oare – say ɔː(r), Bagworthy River – say ˈbædʒəri.

The People in This Story

John Ridd
dʒɒn rɪd

Jan Fry
dʒæn fraɪ

Mrs Ridd
'mɪsɪz rɪd

Annie Ridd
'æni rɪd

Tom Faggus
tom 'fægəs

Lorna Doone
'lɔːnə duːn

Sir Ensor Doone
sɜː(r) 'ensə duːn

Carver Doone
'kɑːvə duːn

Gwenny
'gweni

Jeremy Stickles
'dʒerəmi 'stɪklz

Judge Jeffreys
dʒʌdʒ 'dʒefrɪz

Lord Brandir
lɔːd 'brændɪə

King James
kɪŋ dʒeɪmz

Queen Mary
kwiːn 'meəri

6

1

My Story Begins

My name is John Ridd and I am a farmer. I live in the village of Oare, in the county of Somerset. Oare is on Exmoor – a wild part of Somerset. The Ridds have been farmers here for hundreds of years.

My story begins in the town of Tiverton, in November, 1673. I was twelve years old then, and I was living at my school. I lived at the school for most of the year, but I went home for the holidays.

It was five o'clock on the afternoon of the 29th November. There were no more lessons that day. I was standing by the school door. Suddenly, I saw Jan Fry. Jan worked on our farm at Oare. But that afternoon, he was waiting outside the school gates. He was sitting on his horse. And my horse was standing beside his horse.

'Why are you here today, Jan?' I asked him. 'The school holiday will begin in two weeks' time.'

'Yes, I know that, Master John,' he said quietly. 'But you must come home tomorrow. I will stay here tonight. We will start our journey in the morning.'

'But why have you come for me, Jan?' I asked him. 'My father always takes me home from school at the beginning of the holiday. Why isn't father here?'

Jan did not look at me.

'He's – He's very busy today,' he replied.

But I did not believe him.

———

The journey from Tiverton to Oare was difficult and long. At noon, we stopped at the town of Dulverton. We had a meal there and our horses rested for an hour. Then we continued our journey.

Outside Dulverton, we saw a fine coach. Four horses were pulling it and three people were sitting inside it. One of these people was a woman with black hair and dark eyes. Next to her sat a pretty little girl with long dark hair. The third person in the coach was a lady – a very beautiful lady. She was wearing fine clothes.

'Who are those people?' I asked myself. 'Is the black-haired woman a servant? And is the pretty little girl the beautiful lady's daughter?'

In the afternoon, thick fog came down. We could not see the road clearly. Everything was silent. But Jan and I rode on across the moor.

After some time, Jan spoke.

'We must be very quiet now, Master John,' he said. And I knew the reason for this. We were near our home. But we were also near Doone Valley.

The Doones were terrible people! They were a family of robbers and murderers. They lived in a lonely valley on Exmoor. And their valley was a dangerous place!

After a few minutes, Jan spoke again.

Suddenly, the fog went away.

One rider was holding a child – a little girl. She was wearing a fine dress. I could not see her face. But she was unhappy. She was crying.

Suddenly, I was angry. I stood up and I shouted at the riders. Two of the men turned and looked at me. One of them pointed his gun at me. But the other man put his hand on his friend's arm. And after a moment, the men rode on.

'You were very foolish, Master John,' Jan said. 'The Doones are dangerous men!'

We rode on to our farm. We got off our horses. But my father did not come out of the house. Then I heard my mother crying. And then I knew everything. My father was dead!

2

The Doones

The Doones had murdered my father. That evening, Jan Fry told me about it.

Father had been returning to Oare from Porlock, with six other farmers. Early in the morning, they were riding through a forest. Suddenly, a man rode out of the trees. He was one of the Doones.

'Give me all your money!' the man said to the farmers.

The other farmers were afraid of the Doones. They quickly gave the man their money. But Father was not afraid. He rode his horse towards the man and he lifted his stick. At that moment, there was a shout, and twelve more Doones rode out of the trees.

My father was a brave man and he tried to fight the Doones. But one of them – Carver Doone – had a gun. He shot my father and killed him.

———

After my father's funeral, my mother went to Doone Valley. There was a high wall at the end of the valley. And there was a gate in the wall – the Doone Gate. Two men always guarded the gate. My mother spoke to the guards.

'Take me to Sir Ensor Doone,' she said.

One of the guards took my mother to Sir Ensor's house in the valley.

Sir Ensor Doone was the head of the Doone family. He was a very old man.

'Why have you come here, Mrs Ridd?' Sir Ensor asked my mother.

'One of your men killed my husband,' my mother replied. 'Do you know about this?'

'My men are sometimes wild,' Sir Ensor said. 'But they don't kill people. I don't believe your story.'

The old man went to the door of the house, and he shouted to someone. After a minute, another person came in. He was a grey-haired man with a long beard.

'Listen to this woman's story,' Sir Ensor said.

Mother told the story again.

'That story is not true,' said the grey-haired man. 'Four of our young men went to Porlock that day – only four! Some farmers attacked them in the forest. One of the farmers – a big, strong man – knocked three of our men to the ground. He was going to kill them! Then Carver used his gun. He had to kill the farmer.'

Sir Ensor Doone believed the man's story. My mother returned home sadly.

After my father's death, I did not go back to school. I lived on the farm with my mother and my sister, Annie. But I took my father's gun and I used it every day. After a few weeks, I could shoot well.

Everybody was frightened of the Doones. Carver Doone had killed my father, but nobody had punished him.

'One day, I will kill him,' I said to myself.

———

Many years later, I heard more about the Doones.

Sir Ensor Doone had come to Exmoor from Scotland in 1640. Before that, Sir Ensor and his cousin, Lord Dugal, had owned a lot of land in Scotland. But the two men were not friends. They argued about the land. They went to the law courts in London. There was a trial, and Sir Ensor lost all his land.

After the trial, Sir Ensor and his family came to Exmoor. They built their houses in a lonely valley.

At first, there were only twelve Doones. And at first, the farmers of Exmoor were their friends. The farmers took them food. They tried to help the family. But soon, Sir Ensor's sons grew big and strong. Then they began to steal from the farmers. They stole their animals. And sometimes they stole the farmers' daughters too. They took the girls and married them.

Soon, everybody on Exmoor hated the Doones!

3

Lorna

In February 1676, I was fourteen years old. And one sunny February afternoon, I went fishing.

The Lynn River passed near our farm. And two miles from the farm, Bagworthy Water and the Lynn River joined together. That was a good place for fishing. I often caught loach there. Loach are small, delicious fish. We all liked to eat them.

That February afternoon, I went to my fishing-place and I sat on the river bank. But I was not lucky. After two hours, I had not caught any fish.

I got up, and I began to walk along the bank of the Lynn River. I was walking towards Doone Valley. After a mile, the banks of the river were very steep. Then I had to walk in the water. The water was very cold under the dark trees. But soon, I caught a few loach. After that, I walked on again, along the river.

After another mile, I came to a large pool in the river. On one side of the pool there was a high rock. A stream of clear water fell from the top of the rock down into the pool. And suddenly, I wanted to climb to the top of that rock!

I started climbing. The rock was steep and wet. Once, I fell back into the deep pool. I had to start climbing again. At last, I got to the top of the rock, and I was in a beautiful green valley. But I had injured my foot and I was very tired. I lay on the grass and I shut my eyes.

When I opened my eyes again, I saw a young girl beside me. She was about eight years old.

'What's your name?' she asked. 'How did you get into the valley?' She had a sweet voice, and beautiful dark eyes and dark hair.

'My name is John Ridd,' I replied. 'I've been fishing in the river.'

'Oh, you've injured your foot!' the girl said. 'It's bleeding. I'll tie some cloth round it.'

'It's all right,' I said. 'Please don't worry about my foot. But please tell me your name.'

'My name is Lorna – Lorna Doone,' she replied. 'Didn't you know that?' Suddenly, the girl's voice was unhappy. Then she began to cry.

I wanted to kiss her. After a moment, I did kiss her.

The beautiful little girl stopped crying.

'The Doones must not find you here,' she said. 'You must go. One of the men will see you. Then they'll kill both of us!'

'They'll kill us? Why, Lorna?' I asked.

'This is the Doones' valley,' she said. 'And now you've found one of the secret entrances.'

Then she smiled.

'I like you, John Ridd,' she said. 'Go now. Come here again one day. But please, be careful!'

'I like *you*, Lorna,' I said. 'I like you as much as my sister, Annie.'

Suddenly, we heard somebody shouting. Lorna's face became pale.

'The men are looking for me, John!' she said. 'You must go. But you can't climb back down the rock.'

Then she pointed to a place on the side of the valley.

'Do you see that hole in the rocks, over there?' she said. 'You can get out of the valley through that hole. Goodbye, John!'

I hid behind some trees. Lorna lay down on the grass, and she closed her eyes. Soon, twelve men came down the valley towards her.

'Carver! Here's our little girl!' one of the men shouted. 'She's asleep on the grass!'

Carver Doone walked up to Lorna. He was a big man. He lifted the beautiful little girl in his arms, and he carried her away.

After a few minutes, I ran to the hole in the rocks. I climbed through it. Then I ran all the way to my home.

———

Seven years passed. I grew bigger and stronger than any man on Exmoor. I often thought about Lorna, but I did not go to Doone Valley.

I worked hard every day. I did not leave the farm very often. But we often had visitors at our house.

Sometimes, Tom Faggus visited us. Tom was my mother's cousin. I liked him very much.

Tom was a good man. He had been a farmer once, but some rich men had taken his farm from him. After that, he became a robber. He became a highwayman. He stopped people on the roads and he took their money. He took their money, but he never hurt them. And he gave most of the money to poor people.

Tom visited us every month. My sister, Annie, watched him carefully, and she listened to all of his stories. Tom fell in love with her, and she fell in love with him.

One day – it was New Year's Day, 1683 – Tom and I were riding on the hills together. Suddenly, Tom stopped his horse.

'Look down there, John!' he said.

In a moment, we were both looking through a hole in the rocks. We were looking down into Doone Valley!

I started to think about Lorna. I remembered her soft voice and her sweet smile. I remembered her beautiful dark eyes. And I remembered her sadness.

Then Tom was speaking to me, but I wasn't listening. I had seen something in the valley. Something white was moving quickly along the valley. It was Lorna!

That spring, I dreamt about Lorna often. And one day, I walked along the river to the high rock by the pool. I was a tall, strong young man. This time, I climbed to the top of the rock easily. In the green valley, birds were singing. I lay down and I closed my eyes. The grass was soft under my head.

I heard Lorna's sweet voice a few minutes later. She was coming towards me and she was singing. She stopped near me, and I opened my eyes.

There were flowers in Lorna's hair. She was very beautiful!

'Lorna Doone!' I said.

She remembered me – I knew that. But she smiled and she asked me a strange question.

'How do you know my name?' she asked.

'I'm John Ridd,' I replied. 'We met here seven years ago. You were very kind to me. Don't you remember?'

'Yes! I remember,' Lorna said. 'But don't *you* remember something, John Ridd? This is a dangerous place for you.'

Lorna was afraid. I looked at her big, dark eyes. And suddenly, I loved her. I loved her very much! At last I spoke.

'Yes, it's a dangerous place for me,' I said. 'And you are afraid. Please, don't be afraid, Lorna. I'll go now. But I will come back another day.'

Lorna smiled and I touched her white hand. Then we said goodbye.

4

The Sign

Two weeks later, I saw Lorna again. I went into the valley, and she took me to a secret cave near the pool. She told me more about herself.

'Only two people talk to me,' she said. 'One is my grandfather, Sir Ensor Doone. The other is my servant, Gwenny. My father was Sir Ensor's eldest son. But I don't remember my mother or my father.'

'I'm not happy here, John,' said Lorna. 'The valley is beautiful. And Sir Ensor often says, "One day, this valley will belong to you." But I don't want to live with the Doones. All around me are robbers and murderers. I often come to this cave. I can be alone here.'

'Carver wants to marry me, John,' Lorna said. 'He's strong and brave. But he's a cruel man!'

She began to cry.

'You must go now, John,' she said. 'But I want to see you again soon. Please make me a promise. Come to the valley often. Try to come every day. Sometimes, I'll put a black coat over the white stone outside the cave. You'll see the coat from the hill above the valley. Then you must come to the cave. I'll be waiting for you. The coat will be our secret sign.'

I was very busy during the next two weeks. I worked very hard on the farm. Each day, I went to the hill above Doone Valley. And each day, I looked for Lorna's sign.

But I did not see it.

After two weeks, I had a visitor. One afternoon, a man rode up to the farm. He got off his horse.

'I'm looking for John Ridd,' he said to me.

'You've found him,' I replied. 'I'm John Ridd.'

'My name is Jeremy Stickles,' the man said. 'I'm one of the King's messengers. You must come with me to London, Mr Ridd.'

The messenger gave me a letter. I opened it and I read it quickly. The letter was an order from one of the King's judges. I had to go to London. I had to tell the King's judge about the Doones.

I was not happy about this. I did not want to leave my mother and sister at the farm. But I had to go. I asked Jan Fry to take care of the farm.

It was a long and dangerous journey to London. Jeremy Stickles and I travelled for many days. But Jeremy told me many stories. Soon, we were good friends. At last, we arrived in London.

I was going to talk to Judge Jeffreys. But the judge was a very busy man. I had to wait in London for two months. And I did not like the city.

At last, the judge sent for me. I went to his house.

'Who are you?' Judge Jeffreys asked me.

'I'm John Ridd, sir,' I replied. 'I came from Exmoor two months ago. I came with Jeremy Stickles, the King's messenger.'

'You've come from Exmoor. Yes!' said Judge Jeffreys. 'Your neighbours are a family of robbers. Am I right?'

'Yes, sir,' I said. 'My neighbours are the Doones. They are robbers and murderers! There are about forty of them.'

'Forty! Why aren't these Doones in prison?' asked Judge Jeffreys. 'Is the judge in Tiverton also a Doone?'

I was surprised by this question and I did not reply.

'No,' said Judge Jeffreys. 'The judge in Tiverton is not a Doone. I can see the answer in your face. Now, John Ridd, tell me another thing. Do you know any highwaymen? Do you know Tom Faggus?'

'Yes, sir,' I replied. 'Tom is my cousin.'

The judge smiled.

'Faggus is a good man,' he said. 'He has made mistakes, but he loves King Charles. John Ridd, do you and your friends love the King?'

'We don't know much about him, sir,' I said. 'But we want him to be a *good* king.'

'Have you heard about any enemies of the King in Somerset, John?' asked Judge Jeffreys.

'No, sir,' I replied. Again I was surprised.

'I like you, John Ridd,' said the judge. 'You are an honest man. Stay away from the King's enemies. And stay away from the Doones. I'll send someone to Exmoor soon. He will tell me about the King's enemies there. And he will find out more about the Doones. Then we will put them in prison. Now go home, John.'

A week later, I was at home again. My mother and my sister were happy. I was happy too. But soon, I wanted to see Lorna. I went to the hill above Doone Valley. I looked at the white rock. And there was Lorna's black coat! She had left me a sign. But when had she left it there?

I went to the cave. Lorna heard me coming. She was waiting by the entrance.

'I saw your sign,' I said. 'Are you in danger?'

'Yes!' she said. 'I have put the coat there every day for two months. You did not come, John.'

'I'm sorry, Lorna,' I said. 'I've been in London.'

'Come into the cave, John,' Lorna said. 'People are watching me every day now. We must not stand here.'

We went into the cave. I had to ask Lorna a question.

'Do you love me, Lorna?' I asked her.

'I like you very much, John,' she replied. 'But the Doones want me to marry Carver. Sir Ensor wants me to marry Carver. Grandfather saw one of the other men looking at me, and he was angry. "You must marry Carver," he said to me. "I have chosen him for you. But you are young. He must wait." But Carver doesn't want to wait. And now he watches me all the time. And one day, Grandfather will die. Nobody will help me then!'

'Does anybody help you now?' I asked.

'Gwenny, my servant helps me,' Lorna replied. 'She knows about you, John. I told her about you. She knows about our meetings.'

After that, I told Lorna about my journey to London.

I told her about Judge Jeffreys and his plans.

'I won't leave you again, Lorna,' I said.

Then I gave her a little present. I had bought it for her in London. It was a ring with a blue stone. Lorna cried for a minute. But I put the ring on her finger and she stopped crying. She smiled and she kissed me. Then she took the ring off her finger.

'I can't wear this now, John,' she said. 'But one day, I will wear it for you. Please take care of it for me. And now, go home, John. Stay away from this place. I will send a message to you soon.'

5

The Message

Two months passed. It was autumn. I thought about Lorna every day, but she did not send me any messages. One morning, I went to our secret meeting-place in the valley. I waited there all day.

In the afternoon, I saw a big man walking in the valley. He was wearing a wide hat and heavy boots. He was carrying a gun. He came nearer and I saw his cruel face. It was Carver Doone. Was he looking for me?

I waited till evening, but Lorna did not come. I went back to the valley every evening for the next two weeks. Then one evening, Gwenny brought me a message from Lorna.

John,

I cannot meet you in the evenings. But I will meet you tomorrow morning.

Come to the cave at ten o'clock.

Lorna

I went to our meeting-place the next morning, and Lorna was waiting for me.

'Oh, John,' she said. 'I am a prisoner in the house now. Carver watches me all the time.'

'Lorna, do you love me?' I asked. 'I love you, Lorna, and I want to marry you.'

'I do love you, John,' Lorna said. 'But we can never get married.'

———

We met in the cave the next morning, and the next. But after that, Lorna did not come to our secret place. What had happened to her? I did not know, but I was very worried about her. One day, I made a plan.

'I will go to her house tonight,' I thought. 'I will go into the valley through the Doone Gate.'

The Doone Gate was at the end of the valley. It was not one of the secret entrances to the valley. Sometimes, people from Exmoor had to visit one of the Doones' houses. They went into the valley through the Doone Gate. But it was a dangerous place. There were always two guards with guns outside the gate.

That night, I was lucky. I went to the gate after dark. The two guards were drinking brandy and they were arguing. And soon, they began to fight. I did not have to speak to them. I moved quickly past them in the darkness, and they did not see me.

I found Sir Ensor's house. Lorna lived there – I knew that. But which was the window of her room? I did not know. I was afraid and I did not call her name.

I waited in the dark, near the house.

After an hour, Lorna suddenly opened a window. She put her head out of the window and she looked sadly at the moon. Was she thinking of me? I called to her quietly and she looked down at me.

'John!' she said. 'Are you mad?'

'I wanted to see you,' I said. 'Why are you a prisoner here, Lorna?'

'My grandfather is very ill,' she replied. 'He will die very soon. I can't leave the house. Gwenny can't leave the house. The men watch us. My grandfather will die. Then I will have to marry Carver. I'm in danger here, John. You must help me!'

'What shall I do?' I asked.

'There is a very tall tree behind you,' Lorna said. 'Do you see it? You will be able to see it from the hill, outside the valley. Look at it every day. There are some birds' nests in it. There are seven of them. One day, Gwenny will climb the tree and take away one of the nests. Then you must come immediately. I will be in very great danger!'

————

The next morning, I told my mother about Lorna.

'Yes, my son,' she said. 'One day soon, Sir Ensor will die. Lorna will be in great danger. But she must not marry Carver Doone. He is a murderer. You must bring Lorna here, John. We will take care of her.'

And every day after that, I went to the hill above Doone Valley. I looked at the tall tree. One day, there were only six nests in it!

I went home and I waited until the evening. Then I went up onto the hill again. Suddenly, I saw somebody coming towards me. It was Lorna's servant, Gwenny.

'Sir Ensor Doone is dying, Mr Ridd,' she said. 'He wants to talk to you.'

6

Snow on the Moor

I followed Gwenny down the hill and through Doone Valley. We arrived at Sir Ensor Doone's house. Lorna was waiting for me. I put my arms around her. Then she took me into a large room and she left me there. A very old man with white hair and black eyes was sitting in a big chair. He looked at me carefully.

'Are you John Ridd?' he asked.

'Yes, sir,' I replied. 'Are you feeling better, sir?'

'John Ridd, why do you meet Lorna?' the old man asked.

'I love her, sir,' I replied. 'I'm a farmer, and Lorna comes from a rich family. I know that. But the Ridds have been honest men for hundreds of years. And the Doones have been robbers and murderers for forty years!'

I had spoken foolishly! 'Sir Ensor will be angry with me now,' I thought. But my words were true! And the old man was not angry. He spoke quietly and sadly.

'You must make me a promise, John Ridd,' he said. 'You must never meet Lorna again. And you must never speak to her again. Now, bring her here to me!'

I found Lorna and I took her back to Sir Ensor. The old man saw my arm around her shoulders. He saw her hand in my hand.

'You young fools!' he said.

'We'll be happy fools together, sir,' I said.

Lorna kissed me. Then she said, 'I love him, Grandfather.'

'Then be fools together!' the old man said. 'I cannot help you.' His voice was very tired.

I said goodbye to Lorna and I left the house.

A few weeks later, Sir Ensor Doone died.

A lot of snow fell on Exmoor that winter. The snow was very deep, and everything on the moor was white. I worried about Lorna. Was she warm and dry? Did she have enough food? I wanted to go to her.

'The Doones will not travel in this weather,' I thought. 'I will go to the valley today. Nobody will see me. I will be safe.'

That evening, I took our sledge and I pulled it over the frozen ground. I pulled it down into Doone Valley. I went through the hole in the rocks.

It was a difficult journey in the snow. But at last, I was standing in front of Lorna's house. I knocked on the door and Gwenny opened it.

Inside the house, Lorna was lying in a chair. Her face was pale and she was very weak.

'John. You've come to see me,' she said quietly. 'I'm in trouble, John. Grandfather died and Carver wanted to marry me immediately. I said no. Now the men won't give us any food. We're prisoners here!'

'You must both come home with me,' I said. 'You must come now! Mother, Annie and I will take care of you both.'

I lifted Lorna in my arms, and Gwenny followed us outside to the sledge. Lorna lay on the sledge and soon, we began our journey through the night. I pulled the sledge and Gwenny walked beside me.

After two hours, we arrived at my farm. My mother
and sister met us near the house, and we carried Lorna
inside. We gave her and Gwenny some good, hot food.

My mother looked at Lorna.

'Sweet child,' she said. 'You are welcome here.'

Lorna smiled.

'Thank you,' she said. 'You have saved my life.'

———

More snow fell during the next few days.

'The weather will be better soon,' I told my mother.
'Then the Doones will search for Lorna. They will
come here. We must be ready for them.'

But after the snow, there was heavy rain. It fell for
many days. The snow turned to water, and the Lynn
River ran fast through Doone Valley. Horses could not
cross the river. Nobody could leave the valley. Nobody
could come for Lorna.

7

The Fight at the Farm

One rainy day, Tom Faggus arrived at our farm. He wanted to see Annie. And he brought some good news with him.

'I've bought a farm,' he said to Annie. 'I'm going to be an honest man from today.' Then he looked at my mother. 'And I want to marry Annie, Mrs Ridd,' he said to her. 'We will be happy together.'

Mother and I were not surprised. Tom loved Annie and she loved him. We knew that. We were all happy that day. Then I told Tom about my love for Lorna. And I told him about Sir Ensor Doone and his family.

'Lorna and Gwenny live with us now,' I said. 'They must never go back to the Doones.'

Tom left us the next morning. And the next evening, Jeremy Stickles arrived at our farm with some soldiers. He had returned to Somerset some weeks before. He told us about his work on Exmoor.

'Judge Jeffreys sent me here,' he said. 'I am looking for enemies of the King. And I am finding out more about the Doones. But last night, three of the Doones attacked us. They shot one of my soldiers.'

The King's messenger and his soldiers rested at the farm. We gave them some food. Then I told Jeremy about Lorna.

'You have done well, John,' Jeremy said. 'But the Doones are evil people. Carver Doone and his men will come for Lorna soon. They will try to take her and they will try to kill you. You will have to fight them. I must leave tomorrow, but six of my soldiers will stay here with you.'

A few days later, I arrived home late in the evening. I had been working in my fields all day. The doors and windows of the house were locked. I called Jan Fry and he let me in. The women were very frightened.

'What's happened?' I asked them.

'This afternoon, I went into the garden,' Lorna replied. 'Suddenly, I saw Carver Doone standing near the trees. He was watching me, and he was holding a gun. I was afraid. For a minute, I couldn't move. Then Carver lifted his gun. He shot at the ground near my feet. He wanted to frighten me.'

'Then he shouted a message,' Lorna said. 'He shouted, "You must come back to us tomorrow! We are going to kill John Ridd! You must help us!" I ran back to the house and we locked the door and the windows.'

Carver was not going to wait until the next day. I knew that. The Doones were going to come that night.

I had a plan. I told the soldiers about it. Then I spoke to the women.

'Mother, Annie and Lorna must stay in the house with the soldiers,' I said. 'Gwenny, come with me!'

Gwenny and I went into the garden. I hid behind a wall in the garden and Gwenny climbed a tree near the river. I could see her from my hiding-place.

Gwenny watched for the Doones. After an hour, she saw them. She climbed down the tree and came to me.

'Ten men are crossing the river now,' she said quietly. 'Carver is leading them.'

'Go into the house now,' I said. 'Tell the soldiers about the Doones. Then stay inside the house!'

I watched the gate in our garden wall. After a few minutes the Doones came. They broke down the gate, then they rode into the garden.

'Kill every man in the house,' said the voice of Carver Doone. 'Then burn the house. Burn it to the ground! But remember this – Lorna belongs to me. Nobody must touch her!'

I lifted my gun. 'I can kill Carver now,' I thought.

But Carver could not see me. And I had never killed a man. I could not do it. I waited.

Suddenly Carver moved away. I ran to the house.

Then the soldiers started shooting at the Doones. Two more Doones fell to the ground, and the others stood still. They put their hands above their heads.

I walked towards Carver. Two of the soldiers were pointing their guns at him. Suddenly, he tried to lift his own gun. But I pushed him down onto the ground and I took his gun from him.

The other Doones saw this and they started to run away. Two of them got to their horses. But the soldiers killed three more of them. Carver got up and ran to his own horse. He rode after the other men. He shouted at them. He wanted them to attack us again.

At that moment, Jeremy arrived at the farm. I told him about the fight. I wanted to ride after the Doones.

'No, John!' Jeremy said. 'You will be in danger. There are more Doones on the other side of the river.'

We did not chase Carver and his men. But the Doones had lost a fight. That was something new!

8

The Truth About Lorna

A few days later, Jeremy Stickles told me a strange story. It was late in the evening. The women had gone to bed.

'John, I must tell you something,' Jeremy said. 'You won't like it. But you must hear it!'

'Tell me, Jeremy,' I said.

'Yesterday, I was riding back from Dulverton,' Jeremy said. 'It was late in the afternoon, and I was tired. I wanted to rest and I wanted some food. I stopped at an inn, near the sea. The owner of the inn was a woman – a woman with black hair and dark eyes. She told me her name. It was Benita. She was an Italian. And she told me the story of her life.'

'Many years ago, Benita worked for an Englishman's family,' Jeremy said. 'The family – a man, his wife and his young daughter – lived in Rome. Benita was the family's servant. They were a rich family. They owned a lot of land in Scotland. There had been an argument about some of the land – an argument between the man and his cousin. There had been a trial, and the cousin had lost all his land.'

'Benita often travelled through Europe with this family,' Jeremy said. 'But one day, the man fell from his horse and he died. This happened in France. For six months after that, the man's wife stayed in France.'

'But at last, she brought the little girl back to England,' said Jeremy. 'And Benita came with them. The family owned a house in Watchet. The three of them were going to live there.'

'One November afternoon, they were travelling in their coach,' said Jeremy. 'They were on the road to Watchet. They were near the sea. Suddenly, the driver of the coach saw some men on horses. They were waiting next to a big rock. They had guns. They were going to attack the coach. The driver drove the coach onto the sand and towards the sea. He tried to escape from the robbers. But the robbers followed on their horses. The wheels of the heavy coach went deep into the sand. The coach could not move quickly.'

'The lady in the coach saw an old man riding with the robbers. She spoke to Benita. She said, "I know that man! He is Sir Ensor Doone – my husband's cousin. He is our family's enemy!" Then she asked the driver to go faster. After a moment, the coach was in the sea. But the waves of the sea turned the coach onto its side. And then, something hit Benita's head.'

'Later, Benita opened her eyes,' Jeremy said. 'She was very cold. She was lying on the sand and the rich lady was sitting on a rock nearby. The Doones had gone. And the little girl had gone too!'

'Benita and the coach driver took the lady to her house in Watchet,' said Jeremy. 'But she soon died.'

'What happened to the little girl?' I asked. 'And why did Benita stay in Somerset?'

'The Doones took everything from the coach,' Jeremy answered. 'Benita had no money. She could not go back to Italy. She stayed here and she married a man from Dulverton.'

'What happened to the little girl?' I asked again.

'Can't you guess that, John?' Jeremy said. 'The little girl was Lorna!'

Then I remembered the day after my father's death – November 29th, 1673. Jan Fry had taken me home from school that day. We had seen a coach near Dulverton. I remembered the people in the fine coach – the lady, her servant and the pretty little girl. And I remembered another thing. That night, I had seen the Doones riding on the moor. One of them had been holding a child on his horse.

'Who were Lorna's parents?' I asked.

'Their names were Lord and Lady Dugal,' Jeremy answered. 'The Dugals were one of the richest families in England. John, you must tell Lorna the truth about her family. She is not a Doone. She is Lady Lorna Dugal!'

9

'Lorna Has Forgotten Me!'

I had to tell Lorna about her family. But I was afraid.

'The Dugals are a rich and important family,' I thought. 'Will Lorna want to marry a farmer now?'

The next morning, Lorna was sitting in the garden. She was reading a book. I sat down beside her.

'I have to tell you something, Lorna,' I said. 'Soon, you'll know the truth about your family. Will you say, "Go away, John Ridd!" Will you forget about me?'

Lorna laughed.

She said, 'Or will I say, "John Ridd, I love you!" What do you want to tell me, John?'

'I want to tell you about your mother and your father,' I said. 'Lorna, you are not a Doone. Your father was not Sir Ensor's son. Your father was Lord Dugal. He died in France. You were very young, Lorna.'

'Your mother died soon after your father,' I said. 'But she died in Somerset. The Doones attacked her. They took you away from her.'

Lorna's face became pale. I told her Jeremy's story. For a few minutes, she cried for her dead parents. Then she put her arms around me and she kissed me.

'My dear John,' she said. 'I don't remember my parents. I have you, and I want only you. I love you!'

I looked at Lorna's clear, bright eyes. I wanted to believe her, but I was afraid.

I was afraid, but at last I understood Carver Doone's plan. The Doones were the enemies of Lorna's family. They had taken Lorna from her mother. They knew about her parents. But they had not told her about them. Yes, Carver wanted to marry Lorna, but he did not love her. He wanted her land and her money. He wanted the Doones to have the Dugals' land again.

Soon after that day, Tom Faggus and my sister, Annie, got married. They lived at Tom's farm and they were very happy together.

I wanted to marry Lorna. I dreamt of happiness with her. But then something terrible happened. I came home one evening, and Lorna had gone! My mother told me the news. She was angry.

'Lady Lorna Dugal and Gwenny have gone to London,' she said. 'Lorna left a letter for you.'

I ran to Lorna's room and I found the letter.

My dear John,

Two lawyers have come for me. They are going to take me to my uncle's house. He is a great lord and he lives near London. I must live with him now. I cannot say no. But in four years, I'll be twenty-one. Then I'll marry you, John.

Please wait for me. I do not want to leave you. I told the lawyers that. 'I do not want any of my family's money or land,' I said. But the lawyers laughed at me. They called me a foolish child.

My dear John, our love for one another is strong. I shall always love you. One day, we will be together again.

From your own,

Lorna Dugal

I read those words, and I wanted to believe them. But I was very unhappy. 'I shall never see Lorna again!' I thought.

In January 1685, Mother and I heard some news. The King's soldiers were going to take the Doones to the judges. At last, the judges were going to punish them!

But the soldiers did not come. In February, King Charles died. Immediately, there was trouble in the country. Prince James, the dead king's brother, became the next king. But many people in England did not like him. Fighting started in many parts of the country. Many people in Somerset were enemies of the new king. Suddenly, there were many soldiers on Exmoor. But they were fighting King James' enemies. They could not fight the Doones too.

I waited for news from Lorna, but no letters came from her. Soldiers from London often came to our farm. Sometimes, they talked about Lorna.

'She is a famous lady now,' they said. 'Many rich young men want to marry her.'

'Lorna has forgotten me!' I thought sadly.

10

After the Battle

One day, Annie came to the farm. She and Tom Faggus had been married for more than a year. They had a baby boy. That day, Annie brought the child with her to our farm. My sister was crying.

'Oh, John,' she said. 'Tom has gone away. He is going to fight against King James' soldiers. You must find him for me. You must bring him back to us!'

'I can't leave the farm,' I said. 'The Doones will attack it. Carver and his men will burn it down. I must stay here. I must take care of Mother.'

But I loved my sister and I wanted to help her. And I did not want Tom to die. Early the next morning, I left the farm. I travelled for four days. In each town, I asked people for news of Tom. On the fifth day, I arrived in the town of Bridgwater. It was a Sunday evening – the date was the 4th or 5th of July. The town was full of angry men. All of them wanted to fight King James' soldiers. And the soldiers were nearby.

I was tired. I went to an inn for the night. But very early in the morning, I woke up. The sound of guns woke me. There was a battle, and it was not far away! Was Tom Faggus fighting there?

It was about four o'clock. I put on my clothes and I went to the stable. I got onto my horse and I rode out of the town, towards the sounds of the battle.

Soon I came to a small village. The King's soldiers had left the village, but their cooking fires were still burning. I rode on, and after a few minutes, I came to the battle. The noise from the guns was terrible. The screams of dying men were terrible too! Men with blood and dirt on their faces were running away from the battlefield. But many lay on the ground. Most of them were dead.

The King's soldiers had won the battle.

I got off my horse and I helped a dying man. I gave him some water.

Then a strange thing happened.

A horse without a rider came towards me. It pushed its head against my neck. I knew that horse. She was Tom's horse, Winnie! She looked down at me. Then she turned and began to walk away slowly.

'Winnie wants me to follow her,' I thought. So I got back onto my horse and I followed her. She led me to an old building on a farm. I went inside the building.

Tom Faggus was lying on the floor. His shoulder was badly injured. There was blood on his clothes. I quickly cut a piece of cloth from my coat and I tied it round Tom's injured shoulder. Then I gave him some water. He drank it slowly.

'Is Winnie injured?' Tom asked me.

'No, she isn't injured, Tom,' I replied.

'Please lift me onto her back, John,' said Tom. 'She's a fast horse. She'll take me home safely.'

I took Tom outside, and I lifted him carefully onto Winnie's back.

'I'll be safe now,' Tom said. 'No horse can run as fast as Winnie!'

I watched Winnie taking Tom away. Then I lay down in the old building and I slept for many hours.

———

Suddenly, I woke up. There were men standing round me. They were the King's soldiers.

'Stand up!' one of them said. He pointed his gun at me. 'You are one of the King's enemies!'

'No, I'm not one of the King's enemies,' I said. 'I love the King.' But the soldiers did not believe me.

'Take him outside and shoot him,' another soldier said. 'The King's enemies must die. That is the law!'

The soldiers put a rope round my hands and arms, and they pushed me out of the building. They threw me onto the ground. They were going to shoot me.

I thought about Lorna and about my mother. I loved them very much. The soldiers lifted their guns.

But suddenly, a man on a horse rode between me and the soldiers' guns. It was Jeremy Stickles!

'Wait!' Jeremy shouted to the soldiers. 'Don't shoot!' Then he spoke to me. 'John Ridd! You are my prisoner now,' he said.

Jeremy took the rope from my arms and we both got onto our horses. We rode away from the farm.

'Thank you, Jeremy,' I said. 'You saved my life.'

'The Doones attacked my soldiers at your farm,' said Jeremy. 'You helped my men that day. And now I've helped you. But you are in danger, John. The soldiers will tell the judges about you. You must go to Judge Jeffreys in London. You must tell him your story.'

11

At Lord Brandir's House

I was in London for two months. During that time, I met Judge Jeffreys again. The Judge remembered me. He listened to my story and he believed me. And after five weeks, I saw Lorna!

Lorna was living at the home of her uncle – Lord Brandir. Lord Brandir was the brother of Lorna's dead mother. He was an old man and he was a friend of King James. He lived in a large house in Kensington, near London, with many servants.

I wanted to see Lorna very much.

'Does she remember me?' I asked myself. 'Does she still love me?'

Many people talked about the beautiful Lady Lorna Dugal. I learnt many things about her. Many rich and important young men wanted to marry her. And Queen Mary liked her very much. The two women often met and talked together. And on Sundays, they went to a church in London together.

One Sunday, I went to the church. I sat in a corner of the church and I waited for Lorna. After some minutes, King James and Queen Mary entered the church. Many great lords and ladies followed them.

And then Lorna came in. She was wearing a white dress. She was very beautiful. I loved her more than ever.

Suddenly, Lorna turned her head and she saw me. She smiled. Then she sat down next to the Queen.

'She was once my friend, Lorna Doone,' I thought. 'But now she's the Queen's friend, Lady Lorna Dugal.'

A few minutes later, a thin young man with yellow hair walked towards me. He said nothing, but he gave me a piece of folded paper. Then he went away. I opened the paper and I read the words on it. They were words of love – and they were from my dear Lorna. I ran out of the church. I was a happy man again!

The next evening, I went to Kensington. I went to Lord Brandir's house. Lorna's servant, Gwenny, opened the door to me. She was angry with me. I did not know why.

Gwenny took me to a little room.

'Please wait here,' she said.

Lorna arrived a few minutes later. She held out her hand and I kissed it.

'My dear John,' she said quietly.

'My dear Lorna,' I said. 'I love you very much. Why didn't you write to me?'

'What do you mean, John?' said Lorna. 'I did write to you! I gave the letters to Gwenny and —'

Lorna stopped speaking. A moment later, she called Gwenny into the room.

Lorna asked the servant some questions. And soon, Gwenny was crying sadly. But we learned the truth about the letters. Gwenny had not sent them to me. She did not want Lorna to marry a farmer from Exmoor. She wanted her mistress to marry a rich man from London. She had hidden the letters.

Lorna was very angry. She sent the servant away.

'But is Gwenny right?' I asked Lorna. 'People will say, "Lorna Dugal is foolish! She wants to marry a farmer!" Do you want to marry me, Lorna? You will be happy at the farm. You will have nice clothes. And I'll always love you. But you won't be an important lady.'

'John, I thought about this a long time ago,' Lorna answered. 'I want you to be my husband. I've lived in London for a year now and I hate it! The women don't like me. The men are only interested in my money and my land. One day, I will be twenty-one, John. And then I'll marry you. I'll marry you and we'll live on the farm at Oare. Please visit me often until then.'

Late one evening in September, I was leaving Lord Brandir's house. I saw three men standing near some trees. They were looking at the house. One of them was carrying some rope.

'Why are they here?' I asked myself. 'What are their plans? Are they robbers?'

I watched the men until midnight. At midnight, the street was very dark, and no lamps were burning in Lord Brandir's house.

Suddenly, I heard somebody calling softly to the three men. Then they walked quietly up to the house.

Somebody inside the house opened a window near the street. The three men entered the house through the window. I moved quickly and I followed them into the house.

Inside the house I saw a servant girl. She was carrying a lamp and she was leading the three men up the stairs. I waited for a moment, then I went upstairs too. The three men were standing outside Lord Brandir's bedroom. They did not see me.

One of the men tried to open the bedroom door, but it was locked. The man quickly broke the lock. He made some noise, and the servant girl ran away. Then the three men went into Lord Brandir's bedroom.

After a moment, I followed them to the door and I stood outside it. I looked into the bedroom. Lord Brandir was sitting up in his bed. One of the robbers had a gun. He was pointing it at Lord Brandir. The other two men were trying to open a large metal box.

An hour later, four soldiers came to the house. They took the robbers away. Soon, the soldiers found out about the three men. They were enemies of Lord Brandir. And they were enemies of King James.

———

The next morning, Lord Brandir told the King my story. And that afternoon, the King sent for me. I went to his palace and a servant took me to a beautiful room. The King and Queen were there. They smiled at me.

'You are the great John Ridd!' said Queen Mary. 'Lady Lorna Dugal has told me about you.'

'John Ridd,' said the King. 'I thank you. You've done a great thing for me and for your country. And you've done a great thing for my friend, Lord Brandir.'

Then King James lifted a sword and he touched my shoulder with it.

'From this moment, your name will be Sir John Ridd,' he said.

12

We Attack the Doones

I left London after two months. I did not want to leave Lorna there. But I was worried about the farm. I wanted to go home. I wanted to see my mother and Jan Fry. And I wanted to see Annie, Tom and their son.

In December, I was at home on the farm. My family was happy and I was happy too. And I wrote to Lorna very often. But that winter, there was more trouble on Exmoor. The Doones were making the trouble.

Christopher Badcock was one of our neighbours. He was a farmer and he was a good man. One day in February, something terrible happened to his family. Carver and some of the other Doones went to the Badcocks' house. Christopher was not there. He was working in his fields. But Christopher's wife was in the house with her young baby. Carver Doone pulled the baby from her arms and he threw it onto the hard floor. The baby died immediately. Then the Doones took all the food and the money from the house. And they took Christopher's wife away with them.

The men from the farms and villages on the moor were very angry. Some of them came to my farm.

'We must stop this robbing and killing,' they said. 'We are going to attack the Doones. We want you to lead us, John.'

Tom Faggus joined us. He had a plan.

'The Doones like gold,' he said. 'They like it very much! We'll tell them a story about some gold. We'll say, "There's a lot of gold in the mine at Wizard's Cave. Four men are going to take it across Exmoor on Friday night." The Doones will want that gold. Some of them will go to the mine late on Friday afternoon. And some of our men will be waiting for them.'

'Then I and some of the other farmers will attack the Doone Gate,' said Tom. 'There won't be many Doones in the houses in the valley. Most of them will be at the mine. But some of the men in the houses will run to the Doone Gate. They will try to help the guards there. At the same time, John and the rest of our men will attack the houses in the valley.'

'You must attack the valley from the High Rock, John,' Tom said. 'You know that place. The water falls into the pool there. You first met Lorna there. Your men must burn all the Doones' houses. The Doones must leave Exmoor for ever – alive or dead!'

It was a good plan. We started to tell people about the gold. And soon, the Doones had heard about it!

———

On Friday night, Jan Fry took his gun and he went to the hill above Doone Valley. He was listening for the sound of the fighting at Doone Gate. Soon, he heard it. Then he fired his gun. I was with some of our neighbours at the bottom of the High Rock. We heard Jan's gun and we started to climb the rock.

We moved quickly forward into the valley. We ran between the trees, and the Doones did not see us coming. The men in the houses tried to fight us, but we quickly killed them. Then we took all the women and children outside and we burnt the houses.

Soon the valley was full of smoke and fire. Some of the Doones were fighting our men at the Doone Gate. They saw the flames and they ran back towards their houses. My men began shooting at them. There was a long and terrible fight, but we killed them all.

Later, I heard the story of the battle at Wizard's Cave. Carver Doone was there with some of his men. Our men killed all the others, but Carver hid in the mine. Then he rode away on his horse.

In the three battles of that night, the Doones killed ten of our men. But more than forty Doones died. In the morning, Carver was the only one of the Doone men alive.

13

Lorna Comes Home

In the spring, Lorna returned to Exmoor. She was happy, and I was happy too. And Lorna had some news for us. Lord Brandir had died. Judge Jeffreys was taking care of her. And the judge had made a decision.

'Lorna must marry Sir John Ridd,' the judge had said. 'They will be married immediately!'

The happy day came. I was going to marry Lorna at Oare Church.

She came into the church in a beautiful white dress. I had always loved Lorna. And on that day, I loved her more than my life!

I looked into Lorna's dark eyes. She smiled at me. We made our marriage promises, and at last, Lorna was my wife. She was not Lorna Doone, and she was not Lady Lorna Dugal. She was Lady Lorna Ridd.

I took her in my arms and I kissed her.

But at that moment, somebody fired a gun. Lorna fell down at my feet and her red blood ran across the floor. She tried to speak. Then she was silent.

I ran out of the church. I was mad with anger.

'Somebody has killed my dear wife!' I shouted. 'And that person is going to die too!'

My horse was outside the church. I jumped onto it and I rode onto the moor. I was going to find the murderer. Who was he? I knew the truth. I was looking for Carver Doone!

I rode fast, and soon I saw Carver on his big black horse. He was riding towards the sea. But his horse was tired. I pulled a heavy branch from a tree and I rode on after him.

Soon, Carver turned his horse and he rode into a little valley.

'There's no way out of there,' I thought. 'There is a bog at the end of that valley. I will catch him now!'

I followed Carver into the valley, and suddenly he saw the bog in front of him. He stopped his horse. Then he turned and he fired his gun at me. The bullet hit me, but it did not stop me. I rode straight towards Carver and I hit his horse with the branch. The horse and its rider fell to the ground.

I jumped off my horse. Carver got up from the ground. I hit him across the face. He jumped forward and he put his arms around my body. He was very strong, but I was stronger. I put my hands round his neck and I threw him away from me. He fell to the ground again.

'You are a murderer!' I shouted. 'You killed my father and now you have killed my wife. The killing must stop! I'm not going to kill you, Carver Doone. But you must leave Exmoor today, and you must never come back!'

Carver tried to stand up, but his feet were in the black bog. The soft ground began to pull him down.

Carver fell onto his back. I could not help him. I could not save him. I watched the thick black bog pulling him down. After a minute, he had gone.

I rode back to the church. My mother was waiting for me.

'He's dead,' I told my mother. 'Carver killed Father and he killed Lorna. Now Carver is dead too. And now I want to see my dear wife. She is dead, but she belongs to me.'

'John,' my mother said. 'Lorna isn't dead. She is very badly injured. Will she die or will she live? I don't know. But you must not see her now. She must rest. She must not speak. But there's blood on your clothes, my son. Are you injured too?'

I looked down at my coat and I saw the blood. I remembered Carver's bullet. Suddenly, I was weak and ill. A moment later, I fell to the ground.

Lorna was close to death for many days. And for many days, I lay ill in my bed.

But then, one beautiful morning, my dear Lorna walked into my room. She kissed me. At that moment, I was happy and strong again. And the world was good!

Published by Macmillan Heinemann ELT
Between Towns Road, Oxford OX4 3PP
Macmillan Heinemann ELT is an imprint of
Macmillan Publishers Limited
Companies and representatives throughout the world
Heinemann is a registered trademark of Harcourt Education, used under licence.

ISBN 978-1-4050-7241-0

This retold version by John Escott for Macmillan Readers
First published 1999
Text © John Escott 1999, 2002, 2005
Design and illustration © Macmillan Publishers Limited 1999, 2002, 2005

This edition first published 2005

Illustrated by Kay Dixey
Map on page 3 by Peter Harper
Original cover template design by Jackie Hill
Cover photography by Corbis
Acknowledgements: The publishers would like to thank Hulton Getty for
permission to reproduce the picture on page 4.

Printed in Thailand

2011   2010   2009   2008   2007
11   10   9   8   7   6   5   4   3